W9-BQT-187

JASON
and the
LIZARD PIRATES

JASON
and the
LIZARD PIRATES

by **Gery Greer** and **Bob Ruddick**
illustrations by **Blanche L. Sims**

📚 HarperTrophy
A Division of HarperCollinsPublishers

Other books by Gery Greer and Bob Ruddick

Jason and the Aliens Down the Street

Let Me Off This Spaceship!

Max and Me and the Time Machine
American Bookseller Pick of the List 1983
School Library Journal Best Book of 1983
Master List for Dorothy Canfield Fisher Children's Book Award
Nominated for Northwest Library Association Young Readers Choice Award 1986

Max and Me and the Wild West

This Island Isn't Big Enough for the Four of Us!
South Dakota Prairie Pasque Children's Book Award Winner 1990
Utah Children's Literature Award 1990

JASON AND THE LIZARD PIRATES
Text copyright © 1992 by Gery Greer and Bob Ruddick
Illustrations copyright © 1992 by Blanche L. Sims
All rights reserved. No part of this book may be used or reproduced in
any manner whatsoever without written permission except in the case
of brief quotations embodied in critical articles and reviews.
Manufactured in the United Kingdom by HarperCollins Publishers Ltd.
For information address HarperCollins Children's Books, a division of
HarperCollins Publishers,
10 East 53rd Street, New York, NY 10022.

Library of Congress Cataloging-in-Publication Data
Greer, Gery.
    Jason and the lizard pirates / by Gery Greer and Bob Ruddick ;
illustrations by Blanche L. Sims.
        p. cm.
    Summary: Jason, Cooper Vor, and Lootna kick a band of Lizard
Pirates off the planet Lumaloon in the further adventures of the
Intragalactic Troubleshooting Team.
    ISBN 0-06-022721-4. — ISBN 0-06-022722-2 (lib. bdg.)
    ISBN 0-06-440481-1 (pbk.)
    [1. Science fiction.   2. Extraterrestrial beings—Fiction.   3. Adventure
and adventurers—Fiction.]   I. Ruddick, Bob.   II. Sims, Blanche, ill.
III. Title.
PZ7.G85347Jat 1992   91-14327
[E]—dc20   CIP
                                                                        AC

First Harper Trophy edition, 1993.

To Marla

—CHAPTER—

1

"Hey, Jason! I've got to talk to you!"

I looked up. Oh, no! It was Jennifer McBride, and she was hurrying across the library toward me.

There was no time to lose.

I tucked my book under my arm and dived into the science section. Keeping low, I zigzagged between the shelves. I cut left at the sports books. I swerved right at the mysteries. I squeezed past the water fountain and headed out across the reading area. I was moving fast.

Suddenly, Jennifer stepped out in front of me. I almost crashed into her.

"Hi, Jason," she said, smiling sweetly. "In a hurry?"

"Oh, hi, Jennifer," I said. "Uh, yeah, actually I *am* in a hurry." I sat down at one of the tables and opened my book. "I have to read this book."

I knew what Jennifer wanted. The same thing she always wanted. Me. To be in one of her plays.

Jennifer is in my class at school, and every summer she puts on plays in her garage. Or comedy skits. Or talent shows. She uses every neighborhood kid she can talk into it. Then she invites all the parents and charges a two-dollar admission. She likes to call herself Miss Show Biz.

She sat down across from me and folded her hands on the table. She looked at me very seriously. "You'd make a wonderful werewolf," she said.

I stared at her. "Huh?"

"A werewolf. We're doing this play in my garage called *Dracula and the Werewolves*. And I see you as the head werewolf."

I knew it.

"No way," I said, shaking my head. "Not a chance. You're wasting your time. I'm not an actor."

"Make a face like a wolf," she said. "I want to see how you look."

I have to hand it to Jennifer. She never gives up. I was going to have to be firm.

"Look, Jennifer," I said. "Let me put it this way. I can't act, I can't act, I can't act. Also, I won't act, I won't act, I won't act. In other words, I can't act and I won't act. See what I mean?"

Jennifer grinned. "You'll make a

terrific werewolf. We begin practicing this afternoon. You'll have a great time. Besides, you don't have to act. You just have to snarl."

I sighed. "Let me put it another way. I can't snarl, I can't snarl, I can't—"

Just then my communicator watch began to bleep. My *secret* communicator watch. The one that looked like an ordinary watch but wasn't.

The one nobody was supposed to know about.

Bleep! Bleep! Bleep!

"What's that?" said Jennifer.

I clapped my hand over the watch.

"What's what?" I said. "Uh, excuse me a minute. I've got to tie my shoe."

I quickly slid my chair back, leaned over, and stuck my head under the table. I looked at my watch. The watch face was fading away. It was becoming a tiny TV screen. Suddenly, a man's face appeared on the screen. A tanned, smiling face.

"Are you there, Jason?" he said. "Can you read me?"

It was Cooper Vor. He lives down the street from me. He's the one who gave me my communicator watch.

He also gave me a job. A summer job, as his assistant.

And there's one more thing I should mention about Cooper Vor.

He's an alien from outer space.

— C H A P T E R —

2

I pushed a button on my communicator watch.

"Hi, Coop," I whispered. "Yes, I can read you. What's up?"

"A change of plan," said Coop. "Can you come over right away? I think we should leave on our mission within the next half hour."

"Sure," I said. "I'll be right there."

I'm the only one who knows that Coop is an alien from outer space. I met him by accident while I was chasing my neighbor's dog, Ranger, through Coop's backyard. That's when Coop hired me to be his assistant. And right away we went on a mission to the distant planet Urkar.

That's Coop's job—to go on missions. He's an Intragalactic Troubleshooter. Whenever anyone has a problem—anywhere in the galaxy—Coop can be hired to solve it. He'll tackle any kind of problem, large or small. Mostly they seem to be large. *Very* large. And dangerous.

I put my mouth close to my communicator watch. "I'm at the public library right now, Coop," I whispered. "But I can be at your house in ten minutes."

"Great," said Coop. "Over and out."

"Over and out," I said.

Suddenly, I heard a voice. "Okay, if you don't want to be a werewolf, then you can be Dracula. You'd make a super Dracula."

I gave a start. It was Jennifer. She was

peering under the library table at me. I had almost forgotten about her. And her Dracula play.

"A super, super, duper Dracula," she added.

"A super, super, duper no," I said. "You can super, super, duper count me out."

I tried to straighten up but cracked my head on the underside of the table. Jennifer snickered. I finally got untangled and stood up. So did Jennifer.

"Now that that's settled," I said, "I have to be going."

I headed for the door. So did Jennifer.

"Make your voice real deep," she said as she followed me. "And then say, 'I vill suck your bloooood.'"

I hurried outside into the sunshine. So did Jennifer.

I made my voice deep. "I vill go craaaazy," I said, "If you don't leeeeave me aloooone."

"Perfect!" said Jennifer. "You've got the part. Now, let's discuss your costume. . . ."

I grabbed my bike. Jennifer grabbed her bike.

I groaned to myself. Like I said before, Jennifer never gives up. If I didn't think of a way to stop her, she was going to follow me all the way to Coop's house.

Just then I remembered something Coop had told me about my communicator watch. He said it could do a bunch of really neat things. It had a siren, for instance. And a laser. And an emergency signal light.

And it had *a smoke bomb*. For confusing the enemy and making quick escapes.

In other words, just what I needed right now.

I grinned at Jennifer. "I do hope you'll excuse me," I said, bowing deeply, "but I really must be on my way."

Then I pressed the smoke-bomb button.

PSSSSSSSSSSSSST!!!

A huge cloud of smoke came billowing out of my watch. It was amazing. In two seconds I couldn't see Jennifer anymore. Or anything else. I was completely surrounded by thick black smoke.

Ha! I thought. That should confuse the enemy. Now for the escape.

I raced toward the street, rolling my bike beside me. After a few steps, I burst out of the smoke cloud. I jumped on my bike and began pedaling down the street. Fast.

As I rounded the corner, I looked back. Jennifer was just staggering out of the cloud. She was looking all around like she was dazed. She spotted me just before I whizzed out of sight.

"Hey, Jason!" she yelled after me. "That was great! How about doing that in the play?"

Ten minutes later I pulled up in front of Coop's house. I leaned my bike against a tree and knocked on his front door.

Lootna opened it. With her tail.

Lootna is the third member of our team. She's Coop's cat-creature pet, and she's from the planet Ganx. Basically, she looks like a very large, silky black cat—except she has ears like a rabbit and a tail like a monkey. And she can talk, too.

And she started talking the minute she opened the door.

"Hi, Jason," she said. "Guess what. We're doomed. We're done for. We're goners."

I stared at her. "Huh?"

"We're finished," she went on. "We're history. We're going to be eaten by Lizard Pirates."

"We are?"

"Definitely," she said. "And it's all Cooper's fault. Just wait till you hear what he's gotten us into *this* time."

She motioned me inside with her tail and started marching through the house. I followed her.

Doomed? I was thinking. Done for? This was beginning to sound even worse than being in one of Jennifer's plays.

"It's not enough that we're supposed to sneak up on some giant Lizard Pirates," Lootna said over her shoulder. "Oh, no! Guess how *many* Lizard Pirates there are—fifty! And guess what we're supposed to *do*—kick them off a planet!

Now what do you think about *that*?"

I swallowed hard. "Sounds pretty tough," I admitted.

"It sounds rough, tough, and totally impossible!" burst out Lootna. She gave a disgusted snort. "In other words, just the sort of mission Cooper can't resist. By the way, do you know how many teeth a Lizard Pirate has?"

"Uh, no," I said.

"Neither do I," said Lootna. "But I'll bet it's a lot."

I hoped she was wrong. In fact, I hoped they didn't have *any* teeth. I hoped they just had nice soft gums.

We walked through the living room and into the kitchen.

There was Coop. He was standing in front of a large microwave oven, pushing some buttons. Even though Coop is an alien, he looks just like a human. A tall, athletic human—with muscles all over the place.

He grinned as we walked in.

"Hi there, Jason," he said. "Wait'll you hear about the great mission I've got lined up. You're going to love it. It's the sort of mission we Troubleshooters can really sink our teeth into."

Lootna snorted. "Who do you think you're kidding? We know who's going to sink whose teeth into whom! And that reminds me, how many teeth *does* a Lizard Pirate have?"

"One hundred thirty-two large pointy ones," said Coop. "But don't worry. If my plan works, those lizards will never lay a tooth on us."

"*If* your plan works?" said Lootna. Her black tail began to swish back and forth. "*If?* Okay, that does it, Cooper Vor. I'm not going. You can leave me out of this crazy mission, thank you. I'm just going to stay right here and read a good book."

Coop grinned at her. "Now, Lootna, you wouldn't want Jason and me to have all the fun, would you?"

"I'll read about flowers," said Lootna firmly. "Or snowflakes. Something nice. Something safe. Something without teeth."

She turned up her nose and began daintily washing her paws.

"Uh, Coop," I said, "who are these Lizard Pirates anyway?"

"Good question," said Coop. "Most of them are your standard two-legged lizard-oids from the Zeek star system. That means they're big, they're ugly, they're mean, and they're armed to the teeth."

There's that word again, I thought to myself. Teeth.

"Also, they're greedy," Coop went on.

"There's nothing they love more than money."

"Except eating people," put in Lootna.

Coop nodded. "They do enjoy a good meal," he said cheerfully.

Hmmm, I thought. Maybe I should suggest that we *all* stay home and read about snowflakes. Snowflakes are probably very, very interesting. And very important, too. You might say it's our duty to know about snowflakes.

Just then a buzzer went off on the microwave oven.

I glanced over at the oven. There was nothing inside. But near the top of it, a little sign was flashing on and off in green letters. It said: INCOMING OBJECT . . . INCOMING OBJECT . . .

"Ah!" said Coop. "Here it comes."

I looked back at the glass window. *Pop!* Suddenly, a box appeared inside the

microwave. From out of thin air. A big box wrapped in shiny red paper. It almost filled up the oven.

Coop yanked open the door and took out the box. Then he patted the microwave. "You just can't beat these Intragalactic Express Mail Beamers," he said.

Neat! I thought. So it wasn't a microwave oven at all. It was some sort of machine for beaming things through space!

Coop held up the red box. "This is our secret weapon," he announced. "Just wait'll those Lizard Pirates get a load of *this*."

He chuckled at the thought. Then he glanced at his watch.

"I'll explain how it works later. We'd better head for the spaceship now. We blast off in six minutes flat."

Coop tucked the red box under his arm and jogged out of the kitchen. When Coop decides to move, he *moves.*

Lootna and I jogged after him.

Lootna explained to me that she was only tagging along so she could wave good-bye. And to wish us luck. We were going to need lots and lots of luck, she said. And maybe a miracle, too.

We didn't have to jog very far. Coop keeps his spaceship close by. Very close. He keeps it in his garage.

It's a two-man flyer, and it's a real beauty. It's long and streamlined—like a speedboat. There are a couple of swept-back wings on the sides and a bubble top over the cockpit. Also, the whole spaceship changes color to match its surroundings. That's because Coop has painted it with a super hi-tech paint called Startint. The paint was given to us by the Star King of Zarr as a reward for returning a very special energy crystal. The paint is, the Star King told us, the best camouflage in the galaxy.

The three of us jogged into the garage single file.

"Of course, it doesn't matter to *me*," called Lootna from the rear, "but would it be too much to ask what the big hurry is?"

"Timing," said Coop. "We're heading for a castle on a distant planet. At the moment it's nighttime there. If we leave now, we'll arrive at the castle under cover of darkness."

He passed his hand over the spaceship, and the bubble top swung open. He tossed the red box inside.

"And I don't need to tell you," he added cheerily, "how helpful it can be to operate under cover of darkness. Especially when you're outnumbered seventeen to one."

He pressed a button on his wristwatch.

Instantly, the whole back wall of the garage faded away.

And instead of the wall, there was just a giant square of blue. A mysterious, beautiful, deep, deep blue. Like the entire back wall had been replaced by a piece of deep-blue sky.

This was Coop's wormhole into space. In fact, it was the reason he was living in this house, in my neighborhood. Wormholes are hard to find. And they are very handy things to have if you're an Intragalactic Troubleshooter.

By flying through that wormhole, you could pop out almost anywhere in the galaxy. Even trillions of miles away. All in a matter of seconds.

If you knew what you were doing and where you were going, of course. Which got me wondering. Where *were* we supposed to be going?

"Uh, what sort of planet are we going to, Coop?" I asked.

"A very small and very special one," he said. "It's called Lumaloon."

Lootna had been pacing back and forth. But now she stopped dead in her tracks. She turned and stared at Coop with wide purple eyes.

25

"Would you mind repeating that?" she asked.

"Not at all," said Coop. "We're going to the planet Lumaloon."

Lootna stared at him some more. "But that's impossible!" she blurted. "There's no such place. Lumaloon is just a myth. A fairy tale. It doesn't exist."

Coop grinned. "I found out yesterday that it does."

"It does?"

"It does."

Lootna's eyes narrowed. "Are you trying to tell me that the legends are true? That there really is a planet somewhere with *twelve diamond moons?*"

"Solid diamond," said Coop. "All twelve of them."

"And I suppose you're going to tell me that it's a beautiful little green planet?

And that the people are happy and peace-loving? And that they have a fantastic castle made entirely of diamond?"

"You got it," said Coop. "Except they're not so happy now. Not since the Lizard Pirates stumbled onto their planet and took over."

Lootna thought about that for a minute.

Then she turned to the spaceship and leaped gracefully into the cockpit. She sat down in the compartment behind the two seats. She looked out at Coop.

"Well?" she said. "Are you going to stand there all day? Let's move. Let's hustle. Let's get this show on the road!"

Coop pretended to be surprised. "But I thought you weren't going. I thought you were going to stay here and read a good—"

"And miss seeing the Diamond Castle of Lumaloon?" said Lootna. "And the twelve diamond moons? Are you kidding? I've dreamed about those things ever since I was a little teeny ball of fur. So fire up the engines! Let's move it out."

"Whatever you say," said Coop. He winked at me and then leaped into the spaceship. "Ready, Jason?"

I hesitated a moment. Then I quickly went around to the other side and climbed in.

After all, Coop had hired me to be his assistant. And we Intragalactic Troubleshooters are supposed to be ready for anything. Even Lizard Pirates.

Besides, I kind of wanted to see those diamond moons myself.

"Ready," I said.

The spaceship was mounted on tracks

that led right up to the wormhole—and then stopped. I looked straight ahead into the square of blue.

Coop pushed a button, and the bubble top swung closed. Then he pressed a whole series of buttons on the computer panel in front of him. A high-pitched whine came from inside the spaceship.

I braced myself.

Lootna leaned forward eagerly. "What's holding things up?" she said. "Let's move. Let's roll. Let's burn rubber. Let's—"

"Blast off!" said Coop, and he pushed a lever forward.

I closed my eyes as the spaceship flung itself forward into the blue wormhole.

A moment later we came shooting out of another wormhole. I opened my eyes. And caught my breath.

We were high in space, swooping fast toward a darkened planet. Above us were a lot of dazzling, glittering moons. Some were large, some small. But all of them sparkled so brightly against the black sky that they seemed to be throwing off white sparks.

The diamond moons of Lumaloon.

"Wow!" I said.

"They exist!" breathed Lootna. "They really exist!"

"No wonder the Lizard Pirates think they've hit the jackpot!" said Coop.

He made some quick adjustments with the controls. "We'll set down near the castle. Apparently our leathery lizard friends are using it as their headquarters."

"Coop," I asked, "how did the pirates find this place?"

"Just dumb luck," said Coop. "You see, for a thousand years the Lumaloonians have been hidden by their powerful Illusion Device. That device made their planet and all its moons completely invisible to the outside world. Three days ago the Illusion Device broke down. And guess who just happened to be flying by at the time."

"The Lizard Pirates?" I said.

"None other," said Coop. "They took

one look at the diamond moons and began to drool. Then they zoomed right in and ordered everyone off the planet. Weren't too polite about it, either."

I peered out at Lumaloon. It was growing larger fast as we sped toward the surface. At this rate, we'd be there in no time.

"But Coop," I said, "how could only fifty pirates make everyone leave a whole planet?"

"Easy. First, it's a very small planet. And second, the Lumaloonians have no weapons. They never needed any as long as the Illusion Device was working."

Now we were diving through moonlit clouds.

"But where did they go?" I asked.

"They're waiting out in space somewhere, in a fleet of a hundred spaceships.

Now it's up to us. They've hired us to turn the tables and kick the Lizard Pirates off the planet."

Coop gave a confident grin. "Which should be a snap," he added. "After all, we have a secret weapon."

"I'm glad you brought that up, Cooper," said Lootna. "Just exactly what is this secret weapon of yours? Whatever it is, it had better be good. I didn't come all this way to become a midnight snack for a bunch of munch-happy lizards."

"Oh, it's good, all right," Coop said in high spirits. He began humming to himself.

"Well?" demanded Lootna. "What is it? I hope it's some kind of freeze gun. That would be good. A couple of blasts with a freeze gun and those lizards wouldn't be able to move a muscle for two days. Then we'd bundle them into their spaceship, put it on automatic pilot, and blast them right out of the galaxy. Is that what it is? A freeze gun?"

"Not exactly," said Coop.

"Then what *is* it?" asked Lootna.

"It's a party kit," said Coop.

Lootna blinked. "A *what?*"

"A party kit. You know, for throwing a party."

There was a silence in the spaceship.

Lootna and I looked at each other. We looked at Coop. We looked down at the shiny red box.

There was a flurry of claws as Lootna tore the red paper off the box. Then she and I leaned over for a closer look.

On the sides of the box were pictures of balloons and party hats and fake noses and little dancing cupcakes. There was some writing on the top. Lootna read it out loud:

YOUR VERY OWN
DELUXE PARTY KIT!
EVERYTHING YOU NEED
TO MAKE YOUR PARTY
A BIG SUCCESS!
LAUGHS! THRILLS!
GOOD TIMES!
YOU'VE NEVER HAD
SO MUCH FUN!

Lootna clapped her paw to her forehead and groaned. Then she looked at me with her big purple eyes.

"Our secret weapon is a party kit," she said. "We're as good as eaten."

6

Coop banked the spaceship and leveled off low. We were skimming over dark treetops now.

Lootna kept staring at the party kit like she couldn't believe it.

"Let me guess," she said finally. "First we're going to put on some paper hats and rubber noses. Then we'll go running into the castle with our party horns and try to *toot* the Lizard Pirates to death. Right?"

Coop grinned. "We could do that," he said. "But I have a better plan."

Lootna glared at him. "I certainly *hope* so," she snapped.

I certainly hoped so, too. I mean, I didn't want to be a party pooper or anything, but I didn't exactly want to be lizard lunch, either.

"You see," said Coop, "this is no ordinary party kit. This one was made by none other than Finny Ikkit himself."

Lootna's long ears perked up. "The famous inventor?" she asked.

"The same," said Coop. "It seems that Finny got tired of going to boring parties. So he decided to make an *exciting* party kit—for people who want to throw *exciting* parties. This is his Volcanic Eruption party kit."

"His *what*?" said Lootna and I together.

"His Volcanic Eruption party kit. Here's how it works. You're right in the middle of a boring party, right? All of a sudden, you press a button and a volcano erupts! Not a real volcano, of course, but you'd *think* it was real. First the ground shakes. Then there's a loud explosion, like a volcano blowing its top. Then lava fountains begin to spurt as high as buildings. Then huge yellow sulphur clouds rise up from everywhere, smelling like rotten eggs. And finally, even the air crackles with heat.

"Of course, it's all totally harmless," Coop added. "But like I said, you'd think it was real."

"But doesn't it scare everyone out of their wits?" I asked.

"You bet it does," said Coop. "That's why this kit hasn't been very popular. In fact, this is only the second one ever sold."

"What happened with the first one?" asked Lootna.

"It was used at a big party on the planet

Plutan about three years ago. Things didn't go too well. As soon as the volcano went off, everybody thought the whole planet was about to explode. They ran to their spaceships, took off in a panic, and never went to another party on Plutan again."

Suddenly I realized what Coop's plan was. "I get it!" I said. "We're going to use the party kit to *scare* the Lizard Pirates off the planet!"

"Exactly," said Coop. "We sneak in and set up the kit around the outside of the castle. Then all we have to do is sit back and watch the fireworks."

He chuckled. "Well? What do you think?"

"I like it!" I said.

Lootna sniffed. She was trying to look bored, but there was an eager twinkle in her eye.

"Well, I *suppose* it might work," she said. "I mean, I *suppose* I've heard of worse plans."

We flew over a low rise. Up ahead, something tall and graceful sparkled in the moonlight. The Diamond Castle of Lumaloon.

As we neared the edge of the forest, Coop slowed the spaceship almost to a stop. Then we floated gently down through the trees and landed on the ground.

Lootna peered out the bubble top. "Will we need space suits?" she asked.

"Nope," said Coop. "The Lumaloonians keep the planet blanketed with an artificial atmosphere."

The bubble top popped open. Coop climbed out.

"Let's go to work," he whispered.

— CHAPTER —

7

The three of us stood together next to the spaceship. Moonlight from the diamond moons filtered down through the dark branches.

"One of the great things about working on a small planet," whispered Coop, "is the low gravity."

And then he jumped into a tree!

He just gave this big jump and soared high up into the air. As he rose, he did a somersault. Then he grabbed hold of a tree branch and swung back and forth a few times.

Lootna gave a disgusted sigh. "Cooper is *impossible* in low gravity," she said.

After one last swing, Coop let go of the branch. He dropped to the ground, doing four or five somersaults on the way. He landed lightly beside me.

"You'll get the hang of it in no time, Jason," he said. "But let me warn you. It's like eating peanuts. Once you get started, it's hard to stop."

And he jumped up into the tree again!

"Oh, brother," muttered Lootna, rolling her eyes.

Cooper somersaulted back down to the ground.

"It's all in the wrists," he said with a grin. Then he leaned over and took the party kit out of the spaceship. "Now, down to business. Let's scout out that castle."

"Right," I said.

"It's about time," said Lootna.

We started off through the forest.

Walking in low gravity is sort of tricky. We moved in long, high bounces, and I was pretty wobbly at first. But I concentrated hard, and I was getting better fast. When nobody was looking, I even did a couple of somersaults in midair.

All of a sudden, we came to the edge of the forest. Straight ahead on a low rise was the Diamond Castle. It gleamed in the moonlight like something out of a fairy tale.

It was fantastic! It was a castle of sparkling towers and spires. There must have been twenty of them in all. High ones. And higher ones. And ones that seemed to reach almost to the dark clouds. High bridges stretched between some of them.

Surrounding the castle was a huge park, with paths and flower gardens and fountains and ponds. Here and there stood a diamond statue or a diamond bench.

"Look," whispered Coop. "The Lizard Pirates' spaceship."

He pointed off to one side. A big black bullet-shaped spaceship sat with its blunt nose pointing to the sky.

I gulped.

"Keep to the shadows," said Coop.

We sneaked across the park toward the castle, keeping a sharp lookout as we went. There was no sign of anyone. No lights, no sounds, no movement.

But just as we reached the castle, I *did* see a light. Up in one of the side towers.

I grabbed Coop's arm and pointed to it.

Yellow light streamed out of an open window about three stories up. I could see large black shadows moving on the ceiling.

Large *lizardy* shadows.

Coop motioned us down behind a bush.

"So some of our lizard friends are awake," he whispered. "Good."

"*Good?*" I blurted.

Coop nodded. "They can help raise the alarm when the party kit goes off. Now, let's see what we've got."

He put the box down on the ground and took off the lid.

On top was a piece of paper. It was a list of the different kinds of party kits you could buy. Besides the Volcanic Eruption party kit, there was an Arrival of Springtime kit and a Winter Wonderland kit.

Coop began going through the stuff in

the box. There were lots of strange-looking silver things of all shapes and sizes.

"These must be the rumblers," he whispered. He held up some silver discs. "They're what make the ground shake. And these pyramids look like the lava fountains. And these little balls must be the sulphur-cloud pellets."

Coop quickly laid each piece out on the ground. Then he divided everything into three equal piles.

Finally, he took three black bags from his pockets. He filled each bag and handed one to Lootna and one to me. Lootna took hers in her mouth.

"Okay, team," whispered Coop, "let's split up. I'll spread my pieces of the party kit around the park here in front of the castle. Jason, you go around to the right and do the same thing. Lootna, you take the left. We'll meet back here. Agreed?"

Lootna and I nodded.

"And one more thing," said Coop. "Be quiet, be careful, and don't get caught. These Lizard Pirates tend to eat first and ask questions later."

I gave a nervous glance up at the lighted window. I noticed Lootna doing the same thing.

We split up. I sneaked around to the right of the castle and began scattering my pieces of the party kit all around. I worked as fast as I could. Of course, the low gravity helped a lot. I could take shortcuts, for instance. Once I leaped over a high hedge. Another time I jumped across a big pond.

In ten minutes I was done. I hurried back around to our meeting place.

Coop was already there. Lootna wasn't back yet.

Coop was looking up at the window in the tower. He had a little grin on his face.

"I'll tell you what would be fun," he whispered to me. "To have a peek in that window."

"Huh?" I croaked.

But he was already sneaking over toward the base of the tower! I didn't know what else to do, so I followed him.

We pressed ourselves against the smooth diamond wall of the castle. I could hear low, hissing voices coming from the window three stories above us.

Suddenly, Coop stepped away from the wall and gave a big jump. A perfect jump. He rose just high enough to catch the windowsill with his fingertips.

Then he let go with one hand and made a come-on-up motion.

Who, me? Did he mean me?

He motioned again. He *did* mean me. I took a deep breath and tried to ignore my pounding heart. Then I jumped.

I was a little short of the mark, but Coop caught my arm and pulled me up. I grabbed hold of the windowsill.

Slowly we pulled ourselves up and peeked over the sill into the room.

—CHAPTER—

8

Ulp! I thought.

Two huge lizard creatures were standing in the middle of a round room, leaning over a pile of diamonds on the floor. They had big greedy grins on their faces.

Their pebbly skin was a muddy orange color, and they stood upright on muscular legs. Their huge, heavy tails lay on the floor behind them.

And did they have *teeth*! Two long rows of big sharp teeth. Just one of those teeth alone would probably bankrupt the tooth fairy.

Coop leaned over and whispered in my ear.

"The bigger one is Kranga. She's the captain of the Lizard Pirates. The other one is Flib. He's her right-hand lizard."

Kranga was about as tall as Coop and was wearing a silky-looking yellow shirt with a wide green sash. Also, long purple trousers that ended at her bare feet. She had a gold earring in one ear.

Flib was shorter. He wore trousers with patches all over them, a raggedy T-shirt, and a hat that looked sort of like a baseball cap.

The two of them seemed to be having the time of their lives. Now they were wading around in the pile of diamonds, wiggling their toes and snickering.

Kranga bent over and picked up a diamond the size of a grapefruit. She tested it with her teeth. She kissed it. She clutched it to her chest.

"We are *sssso* rich!" she cried. "We've

got so many diamonds I can't even kiss them all!"

Flib grinned a big toothy grin. "We couldn't be richer!" he burst out. "We can buy anything. We are *sssso* rich!"

They cackled with laughter and rubbed their hands together with glee.

"I've got it!" said Kranga suddenly. "We'll buy a hotel! The biggest hotel in the galaxy. And we'll fix it up real good, see. Solid-gold chairs. Emerald door-knobs. Diamond bathtubs."

"Yeah!" said Flib eagerly. "And we'll only let rich guests stay there. Guests with big wallets!"

"Right," said Kranga. "And then we'll rob them!"

"You bet!" said Flib. "We'll get even richer than we already are!"

They went into a fit of giggles and snickers and snorts.

Suddenly, Kranga grabbed Flib's arm. "Wait! I have a better idea! We'll buy a space yacht! A huge private space cruiser. We'll cruise through space in luxury."

"Yeah!" said Flib. "It'll be about a quarter of a mile long. And it'll have an indoor swimming pool. And snack bars everywhere. With gold straws and ruby dishes and lots of desserts. And—"

"And a ballroom!" Kranga broke in. "It'll have a gigantic ballroom with a diamond dance floor. And we'll throw huge parties in space. Costume parties! And we'll give a big prize for the best costume."

"Yeah, and right in the middle of the party, we'll rob everyone!" said Flib.

"Of course!" said Kranga. "And the prize, too. We'll steal the costume prize back!"

Kranga and Flib thought that was pretty funny. They cracked up and howled with laughter. Kranga laughed so hard she almost fell down. Flib staggered around holding his stomach.

"We are *ssssso* rich!" they gasped.

Just then Coop nudged me and jerked his head toward the ground. I looked down. Lootna was there.

She was staring up at us as we clung to the windowsill. I could see her expression in the moonlight. It said, "Are you two crazy?"

Coop let go with one hand and motioned her up. She shook her head no. Coop motioned again. She shook her head no. Coop motioned again.

I could see Lootna heave a sigh.

Then she backed up a bit, ran forward, and gave a big leap.

Too big. She used too much muscle for the low gravity.

She went sailing over our heads and through the open window! She landed right in the middle of the pile of diamonds.

"AAAAAAK!" screamed Flib. "What's that?"

"It's a spy, you nitwit!" yelled Kranga. "Don't just stand there. Get it! Catch it!"

Lootna scrambled out of the diamonds. Flib dived for her. Lootna dodged him and made for the window, but Kranga cut her off. Lootna doubled back.

"Guards! Guards!" yelled Kranga.

The door slammed open and more Lizard Pirates thundered in. Lootna dodged here and dived there. She was like a black streak.

"Shut the window! Close the door!" yelled Kranga. "Don't let it get away!"

One of the pirates came bounding across the room and slammed the window shut. Coop and I let go of the windowsill just in time.

We dropped to the ground.

We heard some crashing sounds above us. "I've got it!" Flib cried out. "I've got the spy!"

"Let go of me, you big oaf!" we heard Lootna yell.

Coop pulled me into the shadows.

"This calls for a change of plan," he whispered. "We have to rescue Lootna. And we can't just set off the party kit. If we do, the Lizard Pirates might take her with them when they leave the planet."

I nodded. "We'd better think fast," I said.

We put our heads together, and a minute later we came up with a plan.

Then we hurried around to the tower door, stepped inside, and started up the stairs.

Coop and I bounded up the winding stairs, taking the steps three or four at a time.

The diamond walls of the tower were lit up by different-colored soft lights—pink, yellow, green, blue. It felt like we were running through a rainbow.

We reached the third floor. Coop pounded on the door.

But he didn't wait for an answer. Throwing open the door, he went striding into the room. I went striding in after him.

The Lizard Pirates were so surprised

they just stood there staring at us. Coop rushed over to Lootna. She was tucked under Flib's arm, and she did not look happy.

"Professor Lootna! Professor Lootna!" cried Coop, waving his arms. "We've been looking all over for you! What are you doing up here? This is no time for social visits! Do you want to be blown to smithereens? Come on! We've got to get out of here!"

Kranga's eyes narrowed dangerously. "Hold it, hold it, hold it!" she broke in. "Just one little old minute here!"

She snapped her fingers, and the rest of the Lizard Pirates quickly surrounded us. Then she crossed her arms over her chest and began thumping her heavy tail on the floor. *Thump, thump, thump.*

"All right, buster," she said. "What's

all this talk about smithereens? I don't like smithereens, and I don't like spies, either! Now just exactly who are you and what are you doing here?"

"What are *we* doing here?" Coop burst out. "What are *you* doing here, that's the question! My dear lady, don't you know this planet is going to blow sky-high in less than twenty minutes?"

"Nineteen," I said calmly.

"Thank you, Professor Harkness," said Coop. "Nineteen."

That made an impression, all right. Kranga's tail stopped thumping. She looked back and forth between Coop and me. The other Lizard Pirates were looking pretty worried. Some of them were eyeing the door.

"Blow sky-high?" demanded Kranga. She thumped her tail twice. "Explain yourself, and be quick about it!"

"Explain? Explain?" said Coop, running his hands through his hair. "Isn't it obvious? I am Professor Cooper Vor from the Institute of Advanced Disasters. This is Professor Jason Harkness. He's the famous boy-genius from the planet Earth. As for Professor Lootna Long-Ears, you've already met her."

From her position under Flib's arm, Lootna shot Coop a hard look. She didn't like the bit about her ears.

"We're explodologists," Coop went on quickly. "Experts in exploding planets. Which is exactly what this planet is going to be in the very near future."

"In eighteen minutes," I said.

"Thank you, Professor Harkness," said Coop, giving me a little bow.

He turned back to Kranga. "Madam,

you must try to understand. Your planet has gone haywire. The volcanic forces are out of balance. The rock core is vibrating. The magnetic poles are spinning like tops. Scientifically speaking, this planet is about to go *ka-boom!*"

"In seventeen minutes," I said.

"Thank you, Professor Harkness," said Coop.

By now the pirates were good and scared. Their orange skin had turned whitish, and they were looking around with wild eyes. Some of them were tiptoeing toward the door.

Flib tugged on Kranga's sleeve. "Let's run for our lives, Captain!" he begged. "I don't want to die! I'm too young. I'm too handsome. I've got places to go, things to do, people to rob!"

"Nobody move!" yelled Kranga. She

gave a big *THUMP* with her tail, and all the lizards stopped in their tracks. "Nobody is going *anywhere* until I figure this thing out!"

Uh-oh, I thought. Kranga isn't buying it. And Flib hasn't dropped Lootna yet, either. This plan needs help. And fast.

Suddenly I remembered something. Something I had in my pocket. Something that might help.

An electronic football game.

I slipped my hand into my pocket. Good. It was still there. My Super-Sport Electronic Football Game.

My parents had given it to me for my birthday three weeks before. I'd played it about a thousand times already, and I was pretty good at it.

I felt around with my hand and turned the game on. Then I pushed the "kick-off" button.

The game made a loud sound, like a roaring crowd. Everyone turned and looked at me.

I yanked the game out of my pocket. I stared at it. "Uh-oh," I said. "My Explode-O-Meter is going wild! I must check my calculations."

I bent over the game and began rapidly pushing buttons. The game beeped. It buzzed. Lights flashed. Little figures charged across the screen in full color. There were loud thudding and grunting sound effects.

The Lizard Pirates crowded around me. I could feel their hot breath on my face and the back of my neck. I was hoping they had never seen an Earth game before. But just to be sure, I pushed the buttons so fast that even I could hardly see what was happening.

"Too high . . ." I muttered. "The rock temperatures are too high!"

I glanced up. There was terror on the Lizard Pirates' faces. "Not good," I told them.

"Stand back!" cried Lootna. She was

still under Flib's arm. "You're crowding Professor Harkness! Give him air! Give him air!"

"Give the boy-genius air!" yelled Coop.

The pirates shrank back. I bent over the game again. My fingers flew over the buttons.

"Four thousand degrees," I muttered. "Four thousand degrees and rising!"

Then I did it. I scored a touch-down.

The Super-Sport Electronic Football Game has terrific sound effects when-ever a touchdown is scored. And great visual effects, too. Whistling, popping, and exploding sounds poured from the game. Fireworks filled the screen.

I looked up at the Lizard Pirates. I tried to make my eyes bug out. "It's . . . it's . . . it's . . ." I said.

Coop pushed his way through the pirates and grabbed me by the shoulders. He shook me. "What is it, Professor Harkness?" he cried. "For heaven's sake, what is it?"

"It's . . . it's . . . *it's going to blow!*" I yelled. *"In only one minute!"*

"One minute!" cried Coop. "One minute!"

He clutched his throat and staggered backward. He spun around and faced the door. "LEMME OUTTA HERE!" he screamed.

He ran for the door, flapping his arms wildly.

That was too much for the Lizard Pirates. They panicked and stampeded toward the door.

Kranga led the charge. She stiff-armed a couple of her men out of the way and galloped past Coop. "To the spaceship!"

she yelled. She was the first one out the door.

Coop flattened himself against the wall to let the other pirates charge by.

Flib had dropped Lootna. Now he barreled after Kranga yelling, "Wait for me! I'm too young! I'm too terrific! I'm too wonderful to die!"

In no time the whole gang of pirates was out the door and thundering down the spiral stairway.

Coop, Lootna, and I grinned and gave each other the thumbs-up sign. Then we hurried after them.

As we ran down the stairs, Coop reached into his pocket. He took out a small silver box with a red button on it.

"Let's make sure they don't change their minds," he said. "Here, I'll just set off the party kit."

He pressed the button.

And as we got to the bottom of the tower and ran out the door, the party kit was already going off.

It was amazing! It was fantastic! The night air was suddenly filled with thousands of butterflies. Swirling clouds of butterflies, of all sizes and colors and—

Wait a minute, I thought. *Butterflies?* BUTTERFLIES?

The Lizard Pirates stopped running. They stood and stared at the clouds of fluttering butterflies. They were stunned.

Coop and Lootna and I stared at each other. We were stunned, too.

"Oh, great!" groaned Lootna. "It's the wrong party kit!"

I gulped. She was right. This wasn't the Volcanic Eruption party kit. It was the Arrival of Springtime party kit!

11

This party, I thought to myself, is in ver-ry big trouble.

There were no lava fountains. No sulphur clouds. No volcanic explosions. Not even a burp.

There were just butterflies. Thousands of beautiful butterflies, swirling around in the moonlight.

The Lizard Pirates looked at the butterflies. Then they looked at each other. Then they looked back at the butterflies.

It wasn't going to take them long to figure out that butterflies didn't have much to do with exploding planets. We had to do something!

I thought fast.

Coop thought faster.

"It's them!" he screamed. "It's the butterflies! They're always the first to leave a dying planet!"

The Arrival of Springtime kit was just getting started. Now the air was filled with the sound of singing birds. And flowers began popping up out of the ground. Red ones, yellow ones, purple ones, white ones. Everywhere we looked, there were flowers.

"Oh, no!" cried Lootna. "The growing process has gone crazy! Even the flowers know the planet's going to blow!"

Now hundreds of silver balloons were rising up from the ground. They bobbed around a bit, then floated slowly toward the sky.

"It's the rocks!" I yelled. "The very

rocks are boiling off! Run! Run! Save yourselves!"

That did the trick. The Lizard Pirates turned and raced for their spaceship.

Kranga and Flib ran too. But after a few steps, Kranga grabbed Flib and skidded to a stop.

"Wait!" she cried. "We don't have any diamonds! We can't leave without any diamonds!"

She looked around wildly. "There's one!" She pointed to a huge statue made of solid diamond. It looked sort of like a giant hippopotamus with wings. It was about the size of a car.

"Let's get it!" cried Flib.

The two of them ran over, stood on either side of the statue, and grabbed hold. Even in the low gravity, they had to struggle to lift it. They grunted. They huffed. They picked it up. They dropped it. They picked it up again.

Then they waddled toward the space-ship with it, grunting and wheezing.

I hated to see them get that statue.

And that's when I remembered my trusty communicator watch. And its handy smoke bomb. Why not? I thought.

I pushed the button on my watch. PSSSSSSSSSSSSST!!!

A thick cloud of smoke billowed out. I couldn't see a thing.

I staggered out of the cloud, coughing and gagging for all I was worth. Kranga and Flib had stopped and were looking back over their shoulders at me.

"AAAAAARGH!" I screamed. "POI-SONOUS FUMES! IT'S THE END! IT'S THE END!"

Flib gave a little scream. So did Kranga. They dropped the statue and galloped for the spaceship yelling, "START THE ENGINES!" Their legs churned so fast they were only a blur.

I guess they were too busy running to notice the violin music that swelled up around us. Or to see the rainbow that arched high over the castle.

The pirates scrambled up the ramp and into the spaceship. The door slammed shut. The spaceship took off. Like a black torpedo, it shot into the night sky and disappeared into space.

Coop and Lootna and I whooped and laughed and slapped hands. We'd done it! We'd actually tricked the Lizard Pirates off the planet.

"I think we threw those pirates a party they'll never forget!" said Coop.

"I think you're right!" I said, grinning.

"I can't believe it was the wrong party kit!" said Lootna, shaking her head.

"Who did you buy that thing from any-way, Cooper?"

"From Finny Ikkit himself," said Coop.

Lootna snorted. "Well, I certainly hope you finny *his* ikkit the next time you see him. Famous inventor, indeed!"

"Now, Lootna," said Coop, chuckling, "you have to admit the Arrival of Spring-time kit was pretty spectacular. Even if it was the wrong kit."

"Hmmpf," said Lootna.

Coop said we ought to be leaving, so we started back toward the forest—and our spaceship. As we bounded along, Coop did a couple of somersaults in mid-air. Lootna and I did, too.

The spaceship was right where we had left it, but it took us a minute to find it. It blended into the shadowy background so well that it was almost invisible. That Startint paint was working, all right.

We hopped inside and blasted off. As we headed back toward the wormhole, we got one last look at Lumaloon. The Diamond Castle glittered below us, the diamond moons above.

"Look!" said Lootna, pointing with her paw. "The Lumaloonians!"

From out beyond the farthest moon, a fleet of spaceships was zooming toward the planet.

"I just hope they've gotten their Illusion Device fixed," said Coop. "If the Lizard Pirates figure out they've been fooled, they'll be back."

He didn't have to worry. Just before we reached the wormhole, Lumaloon and its twelve diamond moons suddenly winked out of sight. And where they had been was just the black emptiness of space.

Lumaloon was safe. Hidden again for another thousand years.

Home again. And as I rode along Cedar Street on my bike, I couldn't stop grinning.

I just kept thinking about the surprise that had been waiting for us in Coop's Express Mail Beamer when we got back. It was from the Lumaloonians—a scale model of the Diamond Castle, carved from a single diamond and perfect in every detail! It was so big it filled the whole "microwave oven."

The Diamond Castle was for all of us, but Coop offered to let me take it home with me. I told him I'd better not. I said

I'd have a very hard time explaining a Diamond Castle to my parents.

So Coop put it on a table next to a window, where it caught the sunlight and sparkled like crazy. He said whenever we looked at it, we'd remember Lumaloon and the Lizard Pirates.

Lootna said she'd just as soon *forget* the Lizard Pirates, thank you very much. But she was admiring the castle as she said it.

As for me, I knew I'd never forget the—

"Hey, Jason! Where've you been? I've been looking all over for you!"

I looked back over my shoulder. Oh, no! It was Jennifer McBride again. Miss Show Biz herself. And she was probably still after me to be in her *Dracula and the Werewolves* play.

She pedaled up beside me so we were riding side by side. She gave me a big grin.

"No way," I told her. "Don't even ask. The answer is still no."

That didn't discourage Jennifer. Nothing discourages Jennifer.

"Okay," she said cheerfully. "So you don't want to be Dracula. No problem. You can be Dracula's father. I'm going to be Dracula's mother, so that would make us husband and wife. What do you think?"

I choked.

"Was that a yes?" asked Jennifer. "That sounded like a yes to me."

"It was *not* a yes," I said. "Look, Jennifer, you're wasting your time. The only way I'd ever be in your play is if it had a giant lizard in it. It just so happens that being a giant lizard is my specialty. My *only* specialty. Sorry, but that's final."

I don't know what made me say that. It just kind of popped out. Maybe because I was feeling really good about the mission, and about tricking the Lizard Pirates and everything. I guess I had lizards on the brain.

"Hey, no sweat!" said Jennifer. "You want a giant lizard, you *got* a giant lizard. Welcome to the play, Jason! Of course, I'll have to rewrite the story a little . . ."

"What!" I sputtered. "Wait! I was only joking. I—"

But Jennifer had already wheeled her bike around and was whizzing away in the opposite direction.

"See you at rehearsal!" she called over her shoulder. "Three o'clock. My garage.

And don't forget, you're responsible for your own costume!"

I groaned. What had I done? Why hadn't I kept my big mouth shut? Why hadn't I used my smoke bomb again?

I thought about going after her. But then I shrugged.

Oh, well, I told myself. I suppose it won't kill me to be a giant lizard. After all, we Intragalactic Troubleshooters are supposed to be able to handle anything.

Even being in one of Jennifer's plays.